DAWUD WHARNSBY

COLOURS
of ISLAM

Illustrated by

Shireen Adams

THE ISLAMIC FOUNDATION

COLOURS
of ISLAM

Published by
THE ISLAMIC FOUNDATION

Distributed by
KUBE PUBLISHING LTD
Tel +44 (01530) 249230, Fax +44 (01530) 249656
E-mail: info@kubepublishing.com
Website: www.kubepublishing.com

**Due to the historic nature of the audio recording,
certain lyrical differences may exist between the CD and the book.**

Author Dawud Wharnsby
Illustrator Shireen Adams
Book design Nasir Cadir
Editor Yosef Smyth

The author would like to thank:
Abdul Malik Mujahid, Adnan Srajeldin, Dawood Butt, Badreddine Hammoud,
Mohemmad Hammoud, Ali Hagi, Azam Javed, Hashim Javed, Amin Kanoun, Issmaeel Lawendy,
Usamah Patel, Zainab Patel, Orhan Kulic, Atisak Khankhet, Abdulkadir Uwwais,
Radwan Allahoum, Yasmin Allahoum, Ron Burklen, Katie Wreford, Jasser Auda,
Ayman Abdullah and Chris Colvin.

Printed by: IMAK Ofset, Turkey

A Cataloguing-in-Publication Data record for this book is available
from the British Library

ISBN 978-0-86037-591-3

CONTENTS

Sing, Children of the World

Walking through the crowded streets of a market in Morocco.
Sitting on a smiling camel in the desert of Arabia.
Chasing 'round the bamboo trees of Bandung, Indonesia.
Gathering brightly coloured leaves in a forest of Canada.

Napping 'neath the date palm shade under blue skies of Tunisia.
Freeing kites into the night from a roof-top in Pakistan.
Planting rows of beans and maize on a small farm in Uganda.
Laying back to count the stars from somewhere in Afghanistan.

Sing, children of the world, come together and hear the call!
Sing, children of the world, our youth will unite us all!
Sing, children of the world, the truth will unite us all!
Subhanallah walhamdulillah wallahu akbar!

Splashing through the pouring rain in a village of Guyana.
Nibbling cakes from picnic plates on a mountaintop in Switzerland.
Tending to a flock of sheep down under in Australia.
Greeting morning with a prayer on the golden Egyptian sand.

Sing, children of the world, come together and hear the call!
Sing, children of the world, our youth will unite us all!
Sing, children of the world, the truth will unite us all!
Subhanallah walhamdulillah wallahu akbar!

Crying himself to sleep, with no hope left for dreaming.
Begging in the burning sun, holding out her hand.
Palms held tightly on his ears to muffle all the screaming.
Sitting where her house once stood, trying hard to understand.

See the children of the world – all the children of the world.
Sing for the children of the world.
Pray for the children of the world.

Sing, children of the world, come together and hear the call!
Sing, children of the world, islam will unite us all!
Sing, children of the world, islam will unite us all!
Subhanallah walhamdulillah wallahu akbar!

The Story of Ibrahim

Father, oh Father, why do you do it,
why do you whittle all day?
Why do you carve those statues of wood,
and fashion those idols out of clay?
Father, oh Father, why do you do it,
why do you bow down and pray?
To all of those empty gods you have made,
when there's such a far better way?

There is only one God,
La ilaha illallah.
Lord of both the earth and sky,
Who knows all the answers
to where, what and why.
There is only one God,
La ilaha illallah.

I've looked to the sky, seen the moon and stars,
come then quickly fade away.
I've seen the sun so strong and bright,
die at the end of the day.
I've seen the perfection of all creation,
in every creature and leaf,
and I don't understand any woman or man,
who denies the one true belief.

There is only one God,
La ilaha illallah.
Who will not fade and will not die,
Who knows all the answers
to where, what and why.
There is only one God,
La ilaha illallah.

People, oh people, why won't you heed,
my call to the straight way?
Your hearts are as hard as the idols you carve,
you listen but won't hear a word that I say.
People, oh people, why put your faith
in gods of gold and wood?
They crumble away, they have no life,
they cause no harm and they do no good.

There is only one God,
La ilaha illallah.
I don't understand why you choose to deny,
that Allah knows the answers
to where, what and why.
There is only one God,
La ilaha illallah.

People, oh people, you've tried to break me,
you've called me a fool and a liar.
But I will not burn in your flames,
for faith in Allah will cool any fire.
So hate me or hurt me, do what you will,
even banish me from this land.
I will pray to Allah that the truth comes to you
and I pray that some day you will all understand,
there is only one God,
La ilaha illallah.
Lord of both the earth and sky,
Who will not fade and Who will not die.

There is only one God,
La ilaha illallah.
No, I don't understand why you choose to deny,
that Allah knows the answers
to where, what and why.
There is only one God,
La ilaha illallah.

Alhamdulillah (I'm a Rock)

I am just a rock and everyday I sit and watch the sky.
I sleep here in the sun and rain and do not question why.
I don't want to be a bird 'cause us rocks were never
meant to fly.
But you can sit and rest on me when you pass by.

Alhamdulillah, *alhamdulillah*, I'm a rock,
and that is all Allah asks of me.
Alhamdulillah, *alhamdulillah*, I'm a Muslim,
and there's nothing else I'd rather be.

I am just a tree and this is the only life I'll ever know.
I bow my boughs in worship whenever I feel the wind blow.
And my purpose in life is to grow when Allah says grow.
And be a home for the birds and shade for folks below.

Alhamdulillah, alhamdulillah, I'm a tree,
and that is all Allah asks of me.
Alhamdulillah, alhamdulillah, I'm a Muslim,
and there's nothing else I'd rather be.

I am just a person and my life is full of opportunity.
I can travel through the world over land and over sea.
But will I choose the path of truth or a path to misguide me?
Sometimes I wish I had a simple life just like a rock or a tree.

But *alhamdulillah*, *alhamdulillah*, I'm a person,
and Allah has given me a choice that's free.
So, *alhamdulillah*, I choose to be a muslim,
and there's nothing else I'd rather be.

Allah Ta'ala

Everything Allah commands to be,
will always become a reality.
Allah Ta'ala!

You can try to hold back the waves,
but they will always wash upon your feet.
Two waters flow with a barrier in between,
the salty sea and rivers fresh and sweet.

Everything Allah commands to be,
will always become a reality.
Allah Ta'ala!

Every leaf that falls off every tree,
and settles to the ground so far below,
only breaks away and sails on a breeze,
when Allah commands it to do so.

Everything Allah commands to be,
will always become a reality.
Allah Ta'ala!

We can try to sow a seed,
so deep and dark within the ground.
Plant it, pat it, scare off every weed,
but no matter how long we wait around,
we can never make it grow, you know,
unless Allah commands it so.

Everything Allah commands to be,
will always become a reality.
Allah Ta'ala!

Wings Against My Window

Wings against my window,
are they birds or are they angels,
waking me for worship
at *fajr* before dawn?

Wings against my window,
are they birds or are they angels,
singing me from slumber?
Soon night will be gone.

I hear sparrows whistle, making the *azan*.
I hear their words telling me I am a lazy man.
"Come fast to pray", they say,
"you will find success that way.
Stand up now from where you lay.
This is the best time of the day."

Wings against my window,
are they birds or are they angels,
waking me for worship
at *fajr* before dawn?

Wings against my window,
are they birds or are they angels,
singing me from slumber?
Soon night will be gone.

My heart, it wants to wake up; my body wants to sleep.
The morning air is brisk and cool; my bed is warm and deep.
Birds, they call me to the way,
"Stand before Allah to pray.
Kiss the dawn and greet the day."
But dreams, they just get in the way.

Wings against my window,
are they birds or are they angels,
waking me for worship
at *fajr* before dawn?

Wings against my window,
are they birds or are they angels,
singing me from slumber?
Soon night will be gone.

We've Scanned the Sky
(The Ramadan Song)

Well we've scanned the sky and we've sighted the moon,
and we welcome the month of Ramadan.
When we'll fast together, all as one,
to help and strengthen our *iman*.

Oh, it was so very long ago, in the holy month of Ramadan,
Allah sent a message to the world, the holy book of Qur'an.
A light to shine for all mankind, a guide to teach us right
from wrong.
First revealed on the night of power, with peace until the
rising of the dawn.

So we've scanned the sky and we've sighted the moon,
and we welcome the month of Ramadan.
When we'll fast together, all as one,
to help and strengthen our *iman*.

As the sun lay sleeping, beneath a blanket of the night,
we rise early to make *suhur*, before the white thread of light.
We're patient and kind, remembering Allah,
all throughout our day,
and when the sun has gone and we've made *iftar*,
we gather together and pray.

'Cause we've scanned the sky and we've sighted the moon,
and we welcome the month of Ramadan.
When we'll fast together, all as one,
to help and strengthen our *iman*.

So many of our brothers and sisters, all across the land,
they have no food to eat at all and they need a helping hand.
When we fast from morning 'til the night, to fulfil Allah's command,
we feel the hunger and thirst they feel, and it helps us to understand.

But all too fast, the moon goes past, our month of blessings now has gone.
But we'll keep its spirit throughout the year, everyday should be like Ramadan.

So we've scanned the sky and we've sighted the moon,
and we say "farewell" to Ramadan.
When we fast together, all as one,
to help and strengthen our *iman*.

Little Bird

Little Bird, where has your mother gone?
Why are you here all alone?
Little Bird where is your nest?
Why are you so far from all the rest?

Allah knows the language you speak,
and Allah can lift you high.
Allah can bring you home again,
for Allah is stronger than I,
Allah is stronger than I.

Little Bird, I wish I could,
understand the words you speak.
I wish that you could spend a day
with me,
we could sit and chat as you perch
upon my knee.

Allah knows the language you speak,
and Allah can lift you high.
Allah can bring you home again,
for Allah is stronger than I,
Allah is stronger than I.

Little Bird, I'd love to take you home,
Little Bird, your eyes enchant me so.
Smiling moons in the dark night sky,
I wish that I could lift you up to fly.

Allah knows the language you speak,
and Allah can lift you high.
Allah can bring you home again,
for Allah is stronger than I,
Allah is stronger than I.

I'll tell you a secret my Little Bird,
sometimes I feel alone just like you.
But we should always know, Allah is nearby,
to hear each word we pray and kiss each tear we cry.

Allah knows the language we speak,
and Allah will lift us high.
Allah will bring us home again,
for Allah is stronger than you and I.
Allah is stronger than I.

Colours of Islam

Allah made us all a different shade and colour.
Nations and tribes recognise one another.
'Cause every single person is your sister and brother.
So many different colours of islam.

Fill the world with colour, paint it everywhere you go.
Paint everything you see, and tell everyone you know.
Qur'an will be your paint, and your brush will be *iman*,
so fill the world with colour, every colour of islam.

Truth as clear and blue as the sky we walk under.
Love as bright and loud as the lightning and thunder.
Peace as pure and white as the moon, so full of wonder.
So many different colours of islam!

Fill the world with colour, paint it everywhere you go.
Paint everything you see, and tell everyone you know.
Qur'an will be your paint, and your brush will be *iman*,
so fill the world with colour, every colour of islam.

Smiles, warm and shining, like the sun upon our faces.
Hope as rich and green as the trees of an oasis.
The colours of islam bloom in so many places.
So many different colours of islam.

Fill the world with colour, paint it everywhere you go.
Paint everything you see, and tell everyone you know.
Qur'an will be your paint, and your brush will be *iman*,
so fill the world with colour, every colour of islam.

Hear Me Beat My Drum

The rhythm of your breathing is so soft,
as you lay up in your beds so sweetly dreaming.
Through your windows, smells of bread and sounds of
drumming drift and waft,
to fill your nose and ear,
and tell you that the dawn is near.

Wrapped up like baked pastries in your sheets,
I know you're tucked away so warm and cozy.
There's tea and dates and sweets, a *suhur* party in the streets,
so get up out of bed!
Come and greet the day ahead!

Hear me beat my drum, as down your street I come.
The moon is falling, I am calling,
to wake you for the day that's on her way.
Get yourselves out of bed, before the night is gone,
to welcome a new day of Ramadan.

Our busy little lives can make us crazy,
and it's so easy to get stuck in a routine.
Doing everything the same way everyday can make us lazy,
so let's take control today,
live our lives in a new way.

So wake up! Stop you're dreaming.
Let us wake the neighbourhood,
to share in all that's good, the pots of *ful* are steaming.
Let's break our dull routine,
let all the world join in the scene.

Hear me beat my drum,
as down your street I come.
The moon is falling, I am calling,
to wake you for the day that's on her way.
Get yourselves out of bed, before the night is gone,
to welcome a new day of Ramadan.

Glossary

Alhamdulillah – 'All praise is to God'. (Arabic)

Allah – 'The God'. (Arabic)

Azan – The Islamic call to worship. (Arabic)

Iman – 'Faith'. (Arabic)

Fajr – 'Dawn'. (Arabic)

Ful – *Ful Medammis*. A dish prepared with fava beans, olive oil, lemon juice, parsley, onion and garlic. Commonly eaten for breakfast in Egypt, Syria and Sudan. (Arabic)

La ilaha illallah – 'There is no god, but The God'. (Arabic)

Muslim – One who is engaged in acts of 'wilful surrender' or 'wilful submission' to God; the action of 'entering into peace'. The Arabic word 'muslim' stems from the root letters *s-l-m (salam)*, meaning 'peace'. (Arabic)

Qur'an – '(The) Recitation' or 'That which is to be recited', in reference to the collected recitations of Muhammad, upon whom be peace, described within as being a revelation from God. (Arabic)

Ramadan – The ninth month of the lunar calendar. The Qur'an decrees this a 'sacred month' to be a period of worship and fasting for believers. (Arabic)

Subhanallah walhamdulilah wallahu akbar – 'The God is holy, and The God is praised and The God is most great.' (Arabic)

Suhur – The meal taken pre-dawn before one begins a day of fasting. (Arabic)

34

About the Author

Dawud Wharnsby was born in Canada in 1972. He has been writing stories, songs and poems for people of all ages for many years. When he is not travelling to sing with audiences around the world, he loves being with his family – hiking in the mountains near his home, growing vegetables and fixing things that get broken around the house. Dawud loves adventures and being outdoors so much that he is an official Ambassador for Scouting (UK), encouraging young people to take care of the earth and build strong communities. The Wharnsby family lives seasonally between their homes in Pakistan, Canada and the United States.

Royalties from sales of *Colours of Islam* go to a trust fund supporting educational initiatives for children, directly overseen by the author.

Learn more about Dawud Wharnsby by visiting **www.wharnsby.com**